MR. MUDDLE'S
Good Catch

Original concept by Roger Hargreaves
Illustrated and written by Adam Hargreaves

MR. MEN   LITTLE MISS
MR. MEN™ LITTLE MISS™ © THOIP (a SANRIO company)

Mr Muddle's Good Catch © 2014 THOIP (a Sanrio company)
Printed and published under licence from Price Stern Sloan, Inc., Los Angeles.
First published in France 1997 by Hachette Livre
This edition published in 2015 by Dean, an imprint of Egmont UK Limited,
The Yellow Building, 1 Nicholas Road, London W11 4AN

ISBN 978 0 6035 7191 6
63571/1
Printed in Great Britain

On this particular day, Mr Muddle was in a very good mood. Little Miss Scatterbrain had invited him to go fishing by the sea.

Before he left, he sat down at his table and tried to write a list of all the things he would need.

I'm sure you're surprised to hear that Mr Muddle wrote a list. I was.

Perhaps Mr Muddle had decided that he'd had enough of making a terribly muddly muddle of everything?

As he set out to the buy the things that he needed for a day's fishing, he began to sing a favourite song.

"Five little fish went … went what? Went up the hill to fetch a pail of water? No, to buy a currant bun with sugar on the top, perhaps?"

Ah no, it doesn't seem as though Mr Muddle had stopped making a terribly muddly muddle of everything, does it?

Mr Muddle went straight to the fishmongers.

"Good morning," he said. "I'd like some worms for my fishing rod."

The fishmonger looked very confused indeed.

So Mr Muddle went to catch the bus.

When the bus arrived, instead of getting onto it Mr Muddle asked for a cheese and jam sandwich.

"And strawberries with ketchup please," he added.

How very muddled.

Finally, Mr Muddle arrived at the seaside.

"I think I was going to meet somebody here, but I just can't be sure who. What a terrible muddle!" said Mr Muddle to himself.

He thought as hard as he could but he just couldn't remember who he was meant to be meeting.

His thinking was interrupted by Little Miss Splendid walking past.

"Am I not looking magnificent today, Mr Muddle?" Little Miss Splendid asked, not very modestly. "Yes. Absolutely magnificent, I do believe."

"Oh no, I mean, yes," said Mr Muddle, in a terrible muddle. "Were you looking for me, by any chance?"

"Not at all, I was perfecting my suntan," said Little Miss Splendid. "But I have a marvellous idea. Let's go ice-skating. There's a competition today and I'm sure to be splendid and win everything."

It wasn't long before Mr Muddle found himself wearing ice skates and stepping out onto the ice.

"Help me, Little Miss Splendid!" cried poor Mr Muddle, desperately grabbing onto his fishing rod. "There's something not quite right about this floor. It's terribly slippery!"

But Little Miss Splendid just glided away, elegantly.

And then all of a sudden, Little Miss Splendid turned and headed straight towards Mr Muddle, scooped him up and twisted and twirled him high in the air.

She spun him around and around, faster and faster until he didn't know his up from his down and his right from his wrong, I mean his left. In any case, he was terribly muddled.

But the judges thought it was a triumph and gave them the highest scores!

"And now for the next two contestants," announced the commentator, "Mr Wrong and Little Miss Scatterbrain!"

What a pair! Mr Wrong and Little Miss Scatterbrain!

Mr Muddle, Little Miss Splendid, Mr Wrong and Little Miss Scatterbrain were all as silly as each other!

So together they began the silliest ice dance ever seen.

The audience loved it.

Encouraged by the crowds, the skaters threw themselves into a final riot of twists and turns.

And Little Miss Splendid ended the routine splendidly! Flying through the air holding on to Mr Muddle's fishing rod! What a catch!

The crowd clapped and cheered until they could clap and cheer no more.

And who do you think won the ice-skating competition?

It was the four friends, of course!

"We've won the fishing competition!" cried Mr Muddle, as he was handed the cup.

Mr Muddle was so happy that when he went to bed that night he took his cup with him!

He also slept in his ice skates. Because then if Little Miss Scatterbrain invited him fishing again, he'd be sure to be ready.

The next morning, the telephone rang. It was Little Miss Scatterbrain. Do you think she invited Mr Muddle fishing?

No.

She invited him to go skydiving … or was it driving … or dribbling?

Oh dear, what a muddle!